A Spy in the King's Colony

by Lisa Banim
Illustrated by
Tatyana Yuditskaya

SILVER MOON PRESS
NEW YORK

First Silver Moon Press Paperback Edition 1998

For information contact:
Silver Moon Press
New York, NY
(800) 874-3320

Library of Congress Cataloging-in-Publication Data

Banim, Lisa, 1960-
A Spy in the King's Colony / by Lisa Banim
p.   cm. — (Mysteries in Time)
Summary: In British-occupied Boston in 1776, eleven-year-old Emily
Parker is determined to find out if a family friend is a traitor to the
American patriots.
ISBN 1-893110-01-X $5.95
[1. Boston (Mass.)—History—Revolution, 1775-1783—Juvenile fic-
tion 2. United States—History—Revolution, 1775-1783—Fiction. 3.
Boston (Mass.)—History.] I. Title II. Series
PZ7.B2253Sp   1994
[Fic]—dc20
93-42389
CIP
AC

10 9 8 7 6 5 4 3

Printed in the USA

1

BOSTON, EARLY WINTER, 1776. ELEVEN-year-old Emily Parker drew her red wool cloak more tightly around her shoulders. The late January air was cold, even for Boston, and the wind was whipping across the wharves.

"I see them!" Maggie cried, pointing to the Rope Walks below. "There are Father and Sean, and Joseph is right behind them."

Emily followed her best friend's gaze to one of the long sheds beside the wooden piers. A large group of men and older boys were twisting long strands of hemp to make ropes for the big sailing ships anchored across town in Boston Harbor.

"Shall we go down?" asked Emily, brushing back a loose blond curl.

Maggie looked up at the darkening sky. "It's getting late, and there's a storm on the way, as well. But I did promise my mother I'd deliver these warm johnnycakes to Father and the boys. We'd best hurry, or she'll start worrying."

The two girls walked quickly down the pier. "My mother will be looking for me, too," Emily said. "She sent me out to buy some cod for supper, and she told me to come right back."

"We used to have fresh fish every Saturday," Maggie said. "But ever since the war started last spring, it seems all we get for supper is cornmeal pudding, pudding, pudding." She sighed and shook the bright red hair that was spilling out from under her woolen hood.

Emily dodged a man pushing a cart filled with oysters and mussels, nearly running into a woman carrying a child under one arm. The pier was very crowded today.

"Watch your step, miss!" the man called out angrily.

"Sorry," Emily called back. She turned to Maggie. "It must be hard for your mother to make the pot stretch, with so many mouths to feed." The Sullivans had nine children, including Baby Alice.

"Well, we're not much worse off than everyone else," Maggie said. "Many people in Boston are eating little these days, ever since the British Army marched into town and camped on the Common."

Emily nodded. She knew her own family had been luckier than most, so far. "Don't worry, Maggie," she said, trying to sound cheerful. "They'll be marching back out again before too long. Why, with General Washington's army surrounding Boston,

British General Percy himself will be hard pressed to find a good meal."

"Ha!" scoffed Maggie. "The British officers aren't exactly suffering. While their own soldiers and the townspeople go hungry, they hole up in the fanciest houses in Boston, feasting and drinking and dancing."

"Well, there's no way any food or supplies will get through to them by land," said Emily. "They'll be so starved they'll just have to leave town for good."

"That's not likely," Maggie said. "Supplies can still reach them on the British ships that sail into Boston Harbor."

Emily didn't answer. She knew her friend was right. And the British navy was the strongest in the world. How could General Washington ever hope to defeat such a powerful enemy and win independence for the colonies?

Deep in thought, Emily nearly bumped into two British soldiers wearing bright red coats and white breeches who were strolling along the pier. Some people in Boston referred to the soldiers as "redcoats." Others, especially the boys, liked to tease them by calling them "lobsterbacks."

Maggie pulled Emily out of the way just in time. "Really, Emily," she scolded. "You never look where you are going. You don't want any trouble from the British soldiers, do you?"

"No," said Emily, as she and Maggie quickened their pace. "Indeed not. But General Percy has given orders to his men that they must mind their manners with the people of Boston."

"We're at war now," Maggie reminded her. She and Emily had almost reached the end of the wharf. "Do you really think, after what happened at Lexington and Concord, and the bloody battles at Breed's and Bunker Hill, that the British are going to be polite now? They were so sure we Americans would be easy to beat, but our men have given them a big surprise."

"Well, never you mind," Emily said, tilting her chin. "I'll cross the street if I see any of King George's nasty soldiers, and make rude faces at them."

"Don't jest, Emily," Maggie said, shaking her head. "Sometimes I think you don't really mind having the British here."

Emily stopped in her tracks and stared at her friend in surprise. "Are you calling me a Tory, Mary Margaret Sullivan?"

"Of course not," said Maggie quickly. "You're the last person in Boston who'd be loyal to the King." She linked her arm through Emily's. "Now come on, keep walking. My brothers will holler if these johnnycakes are cold."

When the girls reached the Rope Walks, Emily waited outside the shed while Maggie went over to her father and brothers.

"What are you doing here, Mary Margaret?" Emily heard Mr. Sullivan's voice boom. He was a large man with very broad shoulders and jet black hair. "It will be storming soon, and it's a long way home."

"I've brought you some cakes," Maggie told him, bringing them out from under her cloak. Emily peeked into the shed and saw Maggie's brothers gathering around her eagerly. "Thanks, Maggie," Sean said, reaching for a cake that was wrapped in a checkered cloth. "'Twas right hungry we were getting."

Emily smiled. The oldest Sullivan boys never turned down food. They were as large as their father, with the same blue eyes and freckled skin, but Sean's hair was red like Maggie's, and Joseph's was blond.

7

"Hullo there, Emily!" Sean called. "Do you have any amusing stories for us today?"

Emily flushed. Maggie's brothers were always teasing her about the tiny exaggerations she made sometimes, especially when she was excited about something. Her mother just said she had an overactive imagination.

"Both of you girls get along home, now," Mr. Sullivan said. "I won't have you out in the dark, catching your death of a cold."

"Yes, Father," Maggie said, standing on tiptoe to give him a quick kiss on the cheek.

Mr. Sullivan and the boys turned back to their work just as the stern-looking man in charge walked over to them. Ropemaking was a hard, rough job, and the men worked through until nightfall, which came early during the short winter months.

Just as Emily and Maggie were leaving the waterfront, Emily remembered the cod she was supposed to get for supper. "Oh, no!" she said, clapping a hand to her mouth. "I'll have to go to the harbor, or Mother will be angry."

"There's a fishmonger over there with a cart," Maggie said, pointing toward the next pier. "I'll wait for you."

Emily ran over and gave the fishmonger a coin for a large cod. He wrapped the fish in thick brown paper and handed it to her. Thanking him, she ran quickly back to Maggie, carrying the parcel tightly under her arm.

The two girls finally left the wharves and followed the narrow, twisted streets toward Boston Common, the large, grassy town square. Maggie lived a ways past the Common, in the north end of town, but Emily would not have to go much farther to reach her family's house on Winter Street.

"The lamplighter is already making his rounds," said Maggie. She nodded toward a tall man who was using a long pole to light the candle in a nearby lamppost.

"Perhaps we'll need the night watchman to take us home," Emily said brightly. "Wouldn't our families be surprised?"

Maggie groaned. "Don't say that, Emily, even in jest. My mother would be absolutely furious."

"Or even worse," Emily added with a mischievous grin, "a British soldier might escort us. He'd tell our families we were out causing trouble and plotting against the enemy."

Maggie reached out to give Emily a good-natured push. Emily pushed back, forgetting her package of fish. It fell onto the ground with a plop.

"Now look what you made me do, Maggie Sullivan!" Emily bent down and scooped up the package. Luckily, the fish had not fallen out of the paper onto the dirty cobblestones.

Maggie laughed and started to run. Emily took off after her, but Maggie had already disappeared into the shadows of the trees and bushes along the side of the Common. "Goodbyyye, Emileeee!" she heard Maggie call from somewhere ahead in the darkness.

Emily kept running, determined to catch up with her friend. Suddenly, a man stepped out of the bushes in front of her, holding a lantern.

"Halt! Who goes there?" he called in a deep, gruff voice.

Emily froze, her heart pounding in her throat. It was an angry-looking British soldier!

2

EMILY OPENED HER MOUTH TO ANSWER the British soldier, but no words came out.

"Speak up, girl," the soldier demanded. "Has the cat got your tongue?"

"N-no, sir," Emily stammered.

The soldier held his lantern closer to Emily's face. Emily could see the cold, hard glint in his eyes as he studied her from the top of her cloak to the buckles on her heavy dark shoes.

"I'm on my way home," Emily told him, trying not to sound afraid. "I was down at the river, and all of a sudden it grew late."

"A likely story," the soldier said. One side of his mouth turned up in a sneer. "I'll wager you were out running an errand for one of those no-good Yankee rascals. What's that you're carrying in that paper?"

Emily looked down at the package in her arms. She was beginning to feel more angry than frightened. It was none of the soldier's business what she was carrying. She lifted her chin. "'Tis nothing but a fish for my family's supper," she said.

The soldier guffawed loudly. "A fish, is it? Well, hand it over. You've no doubt missed your supper, and there are plenty of hungry men camping back there on the Common who could use a good meal."

"I will *not* hand it over," Emily answered, clutching her package more tightly. "If your men are so hungry, they can all sail back over the sea to England where they belong."

The soldier's face grew dark. "How dare you insult a soldier of the King?" he thundered. "I'll have you thrown in the gaol for this, you impudent little—"

"Excuse me," said a voice from the darkness. A tall figure suddenly stepped out of the shadows.

Emily looked up in surprise. It was Robert Babcock, her handsome, young next-door neighbor. He was wearing a long gray cloak and a black, tri-cornered hat.

"Excuse me," Robert repeated. "But this is my sister. I was escorting her home, and she darted ahead of me. I am sorry if she has been giving you trouble."

The soldier looked a little less angry. "Oh, she's yours, is she, young Babcock? I can see that she is a difficult maid. You'd best get her in before curfew, or there could be trouble."

"Yes, sir," Robert said quickly, taking Emily by the arm. "We'll be on our way now."

"Let go of me," Emily hissed to Robert as

he led her away. "What are you doing here? How does that soldier know you? And why did you tell him that I was your sister?"

"Hush," said Robert, his dark eyes serious. "He might hear you. It's a good thing you're not my sister, or I'd give you a wallop for sure. Don't you realize how dangerous it is to make a King's soldier angry? He could well cause trouble for your family."

"Because we're Patriots, you mean?" said Emily. She sniffed. "Not like your Tory family."

Beside her, Robert stiffened. "It's true my parents and brothers are Loyalists. But you know full well that I am a Patriot. Just ask your father."

"Hmph," said Emily. She couldn't understand how Robert could feel differently than the rest of his family about remaining loyal to the King. But she had known Robert for a very long time, and her seventeen-year-old sister

Caroline thought the sun, moon, and stars revolved around him.

They were almost to their street now. Emily was beginning to worry about what her mother was going to say about her being so late.

Suddenly, Emily frowned and cocked her head. She was sure she heard footsteps behind them. She turned around quickly, but didn't see anyone.

A few moments later, she heard the footsteps again. Beside her, Robert was still talking on and on about the Patriot cause, but she wasn't paying any attention to him.

"Did you hear that?" Emily interrupted.

Robert looked at her blankly. "Hear what?"

"I think someone's following us."

Robert glanced behind them. "There's no one there," he said. "You're probably just jumpy after running into that soldier."

Why did Robert always treat her as though

she were a child? She was eleven, after all, and he was only eighteen! "I *know* I heard foot-steps," she said.

Robert was still holding her by the arm. "We've reached your house," he said, looking up at the well-kept two-story building. "Come on, I'll go up to the door with you."

Just as Emily reached for the latch, the door opened. Her mother, a slender, fair-com-plexioned woman, stood in the doorway in her apron. "Where on earth have you been?"

Emily stared at the ground. For once, she couldn't think of anything to say.

"Emily has been with me," Robert spoke up. "I'm sorry that she has been delayed. I stopped along the way to discuss some important business with a man I know."

Emily looked at him gratefully.

Mrs. Parker shook her head. "Well, I'm just glad Emily's back safe and sound. Her father was about to go out looking for her." She held the door open wider. "Come in, come in. You will stay for supper, won't you, Robert?"

Robert hesitated. "Oh, no, Mistress Parker. I wouldn't want to impose."

"Nonsense," she said briskly, ushering him and Emily into the house. "We'll simply stretch the pot a bit. Emily, do you have the fish? I'll put it on the fire right now."

Emily handed her the package while Robert went into the main room to speak with Emily's father. Emily followed her mother to the kitchen. Caroline was already there, stirring a pot of beans and molasses. Like Emily and their mother, she had blond hair and blue eyes.

"Where have *you* been?" Caroline demanded as soon as she saw Emily. "Why weren't you here to help Mother and me prepare the meal?"

"I was with Robert," answered Emily as she

went over to take her apron from a hook in the corner of the room. She hung up her cloak and put on the apron. Then she looked back at Caroline and grinned. She knew very well that her sister was in love with Robert, even though Caroline tried to hide it. She had a feeling that Robert thought Caroline was special, too, but she had no idea why. Caroline could be very annoying sometimes.

"Is Robert still here?" Caroline asked casually. She pretended to peer more closely into the bean pot, but Emily could see that her face was pink.

"He's staying for supper," Emily told her. "So you can stare across the table at him for hours."

Caroline glared at her. "You needn't tease so! What do you care if I fancy him?"

"He's a Tory," Emily replied. She picked up a knife and began to chop vegetables for the huge pot that hung over the open hearth fire.

"He is not," Caroline said. "Why are you always saying that?"

Emily shrugged. "Well, his parents and brothers are Loyalists. How could Robert not be one, too?" *Besides,* she added to herself, *he had been hanging around the Common tonight. A British soldier had even recognized him.*

"Many families and neighbors are divided over this war," Caroline said. "And most have not decided whether to support the Patriots or the King."

"Girls, stop all of this talk right now!" said Mrs. Parker. She was carrying fresh brown bread in a wicker basket. "We don't have much time to get supper on the table. Your father is meeting here with some of his friends tonight, and we have a guest, besides. Emily, when you're finished with those vegetables, you can start slicing this bread."

Half an hour later, everyone gathered around the table in the main room. The food smelled delicious, and Emily was very hungry. She was so busy eating that she didn't pay much attention to the conversation at the table. Mostly, her father, a well-known doctor in Boston, and Robert talked about the British soldiers, and whether General Washington would be able to drive them out.

"The situation looks quite bleak, I fear," Dr. Parker was saying now. "Washington has but a small number of men. And guns, powder, and cannon are sadly lacking."

Robert glanced at Caroline, who seemed to have been hanging on his every word during the meal. "But I heard Colonel Knox is—" he began.

"That was a delightful meal, my dear," Dr. Parker said suddenly, turning to his wife. "Do we have any dessert?"

Emily looked at her father in surprise. Why had he interrupted Robert like that? Robert was staring at his plate, red-faced.

"Why, yes, I made a fresh apple tart," Mrs. Parker said. "Emily, will you get it for us?"

"Yes, Mother," Emily said, rising from her chair. Apple tart was her very favorite. Quickly, she gathered up the dishes and headed for the kitchen.

The apple tart was on the center table, covered with a tea towel. It smelled wonderful!

But just as Emily reached for it, she caught sight of a face in the window, and she jumped in fright.

A man with a long, ugly scar on his cheek was peering in the kitchen window. And he was staring straight at Emily!

3

WITHOUT STOPPING TO THINK, EMILY ran toward the kitchen door and threw it open. "Hallo!" she called loudly. "Who's there? Who's there, I say?"

There was no answer. The man with the ugly scar had vanished.

Caroline came up behind Emily and pulled her back inside. "What are you doing?" she scolded. "Can't you see you're letting the cold air into the house?"

Emily didn't answer. She was still trying to see out into the darkness. Caroline reached past Emily and shut the door firmly. "What could you have been thinking?" she said. "And who were you calling to?"

"I'm sorry," Emily said. "I thought I saw a man at the window."

Just then Robert came into the kitchen. "What happened? You saw someone outside?"

Emily nodded. "A scary-looking man, with a long scar on his cheek. I think he was wearing a black cloak, but I only saw him for a moment."

"I'll take a look," Robert said. His face looked serious again, the way it had back at the Common. "It was probably just a poor soul looking for bread or lodging." But Emily thought he seemed very anxious as he headed out the door.

"Another one of your silly tales, no doubt," said Caroline with a sniff. "I do hope Robert will not run into danger out there."

"Robert is well able to take care of himself," Emily retorted. "And he's certainly been acting very strange today." She was about to tell her sister that she had seen Robert near the British camp at the Common earlier that evening, and a British soldier had recognized him, but she decided against it.

A few minutes later, Robert reappeared. "There's no one outside," he told the girls. "Perhaps it was your imagination, Emily."

"It wasn't," Emily said angrily. "I saw him!"

Robert and Caroline looked unconvinced. "I'll have to be leaving now," said Robert. "But I'll be back later tonight."

"Oh, won't you stay?" asked Caroline. She blushed. "I mean, won't you have a slice of the apple tart?"

"I'm afraid I must go. I have some important business to take care of," Robert answered, smiling at Caroline. He took his tri-cornered hat and dark gray cloak from a hook near the door. "Please thank your mother for the delicious dinner. And tell your father I'll be back later this evening," he added over his shoulder.

Emily turned to Caroline. "Why is he in such a hurry? And why is he coming back?" Then she smiled. "Is Robert calling on you later tonight? Are the two of you courting?" she teased.

Caroline walked over to the table and began to slice the apple tart. "Certainly not," she said. "And stop going on with all that nonsense. You know very well that Father and some of our neighbors meet here at night. Robert is going to join them."

"Why are they meeting?" Emily asked. "To talk about the British?"

Caroline looked at her sharply. "You ask too many questions," she said. "Father says it is best that you and Mother and I know nothing about their meetings. Now come over here and help me with these plates."

But as Emily began to carry the slices of

apple tart into the main room, she wondered why Robert had left in such haste. She wasn't sure she trusted her neighbor very much, especially after today. What was the "important business" he had to take care of? He had said the same thing to her mother earlier, when he'd explained why Emily was late. *Maybe he's going to look for the man with the scar,* Emily decided finally, *and he doesn't want to frighten us.* Then she frowned. *Was the man a thief? If so, was he the same man I thought was following me and Robert earlier?* Emily shivered, remembering the footsteps in the darkness.

As soon as the meal was finished and cleared away, Mrs. Parker and the girls gathered in front of the fire to sew for a while before they went to bed.

Emily yawned as she worked on her sampler. The sampler was a piece of cloth on which all girls her age practiced their stitches. On it were sewn the letters of the alphabet and a short rhyme. When the sampler was finished, Emily would stitch her name and the date at the bottom. Someday, her sampler would be framed to hang in the house she would live in after she was married. It would show how well Emily had learned how to sew. Until then, the sampler would be put away in a special box called a hope chest.

Caroline looked over Emily's shoulder. "You missed a stitch," she pointed out.

Emily peered more closely at her sampler. Caroline was right—she had made a mistake. With a sigh, she began to pull the thread back out again. She hated sewing. But she knew she needed to be a skilled seamstress to make clothes for herself and her husband and children someday.

At least I chose a cheerful rhyme, Emily told

herself as she pulled the last thread. The rhyme said:

This is my sampler
Here you see
What care
My Mother took of me.

She thought of the rhymes some of the other girls she knew had chosen to display their stitches. Even Caroline had picked a dreary rhyme that read:

The eye findeth
The heart leadeth
The hand blindeth
And Death chooseth.

"So what do you think?" Caroline asked.
Mrs. Parker and Emily both looked up as

Caroline held out the blue serge dress she had been working on. It had belonged to Mrs. Parker, but Caroline had added new white trim and buttons.

"It looks quite new," said Mrs. Parker. "You've done a fine job, Caroline. I'm so glad you could find a use for that old dress. The cloth is not worn, and it looks much more fashionable now."

"It's lovely," said Emily, nodding. "When are you going to wear it?"

Caroline hugged the dress to her chest. "Oh, I'm not going to wear it now," she replied. "'Twouldn't be right to parade in such a fancy dress with the British soldiers in town. Robert says some people are burning their own furniture to keep warm. I'll put it away in my hope chest to wear after I am married."

Emily wondered whether Caroline was planning to marry Robert. It certainly wouldn't

be a big surprise—well, to her, at least. But what if Robert really was a Tory? And even if he wasn't, what about his family? Would they want a Patriot daughter-in-law in the family?

Emily hoped the war would be over soon, and the British and the Tories would all leave Boston. But she had a feeling that it would be a very, very long time before that happened. And what if General Washington and his men were defeated in the end? Emily hated to think about that, but she had to admit to herself that it was possible.

And she couldn't stop thinking about the strange man with the scar on his cheek. Could he have been the one who had followed her and Robert home from the Common?

Emily shivered, even though she was sitting quite close to the fire. If that awful man had indeed been following them, then why?

4

THE NEXT MORNING, EMILY WAS STILL sleeping soundly on her side of the bed she shared with Caroline when her sister shook her by the shoulder.

"Emily, wake up," Caroline said. "I've been calling you for ages."

Emily bolted up. "What is it? Where is he?"

Caroline frowned. "Whatever are you talking about? It's me, your sister, you silly girl. And it's time for us to go downstairs and prepare the breakfast."

"Oh." Emily did feel a bit silly. She'd been having a terrible dream. In it, the man with the scar had been chasing her down a dark street, waving a fish. Robert was running after both

35

of them, carrying a musket. And when Emily looked over her shoulder, she could see both the stranger and Robert gaining on her. Worst of all, Robert was wearing a powdered white wig, white breeches, and a scarlet coat—just like a lobsterback!

Caroline looked in the mirror above the dressing table and twisted her hair into a quick bun. "There," she said, tucking the last few blond curls neatly under her white cap. "I'm ready." Then she glanced back at Emily disapprovingly. "I'll go down and stir up the fire, Slug-a-bed."

Emily gathered the bedclothes more tightly around her as she sat shivering among the goosedown pillows. It was very cold. She dreaded putting her stockinged feet onto the freezing wood floor.

With a sigh, Emily threw back the red curtains that surrounded the four-poster bed.

There was no light yet from the small window. Perhaps she was not so very late getting up, even though morning chores started early in the Parker house.

Emily quickly removed her nightcap and white nightshirt and pulled on her gray wool dress. Underneath she added her petticoat, a fresh pair of gray stockings, garters to keep them up, and her heavy black shoes.

Before she left the room, she washed her hands with her mother's jellylike soap and splashed her face with the icy water that was left in the white basin on the dresser. *I'm certainly awake now,* she told herself as she headed downstairs.

Almost as soon as Emily reached the kitchen, her mother handed her an empty basket and a jar of homemade jam. "Go next door to Mistress Babcock's and ask her whether we might have a few fresh eggs,"

Mistress Parker said. "Tell her our hens aren't laying again, and give her the jam. It's little enough, but I'm sure Mistress Babcock will understand."

Emily looked down at the empty basket. She wanted to say, *"Why do we want to eat Tory eggs laid by Tory chickens?"* but she didn't. Her mother would call her rude, and Caroline would probably box her ears. Instead, she gathered her cloak from its peg.

Mistress Parker sighed as she rolled out more dough for biscuits. "It must be terribly hard for poor young Robert and his parents and brothers," she said. "'Tis a pity when there is such disagreement within one's own family."

Caroline looked up as Emily opened the door and stepped outside. "Emily!" she called. "Will you get us more kindling before you go? The fire is nearly out again."

Emily nodded and walked around to the

back of the large, wooden frame house. The day before she had seen many small sticks and twigs beneath the large maple tree in the yard.

When she reached the old tree, she put the jam jar in the pocket of her cloak and began to fill her basket with sticks. The morning air was extremely cold, and Emily's chest hurt each time she drew in a breath.

Hurriedly, she finished gathering the twigs into the basket and headed back to the house. But just as she rounded the corner near the kitchen, she stopped dead in her tracks.

There was a small, dark square of cloth caught in the bushes near the kitchen window—at the exact spot where she had seen the man with the scar!

Emily ran over and freed the piece of cloth from the branches. Sure enough, it was a square of heavy black wool, the very same material that a cloak would be made from.

Emily remembered that she had thought the man at the window was wearing a dark cloak. And the edges of this cloth were ragged, as though it had been torn.

That's it! Emily thought excitedly. *The man with the scar caught his cloak in the bushes, and it ripped when he tried to run away!* Now she had definite proof that she hadn't imagined the face at the kitchen window.

"Emily!" Mistress Parker called. "Bring in that kindling right now! We've lost the fire!"

Emily stuffed the cloth into her pocket and hurried to the kitchen door. Her mother took the basket and handed it to Caroline, who dumped it onto the dying embers.

"Now go!" Mistress Parker told Emily, shooing her off. "Your father will be wanting his breakfast soon, and I need those eggs."

Emily frowned as she started down the walk toward the Babcocks'. She'd have to wait until she got back to show Caroline what she'd found.

A few minutes later, Emily knocked sharply on the Babcock's door. She knew Mistress Babcock would be in the kitchen, making her family's breakfast. Everyone in Boston rose early to begin working before the sun rose. *Everyone except the British officers asleep in their warm, fancy houses,* Emily added to herself. They were probably all tired out after their late-night parties. She'd seen them herself, in the windows of the finest houses on Beacon Hill—men in red coats drinking and dancing with ladies in beautiful gowns.

"Why, Emily Parker, what a pleasant surprise!" said Mistress Babcock when she came to the door. She was a short, round woman with a pink face that was almost always smiling. "Do come in, my dear."

"Thank you, ma'am," said Emily, giving a

quick little curtsy as her mother had taught her to do when greeting grown-ups. "But I'll not be staying. Mother sent me to ask whether you might be able to spare a few eggs."

"Of course," said Mistress Babcock. "But please step inside out of this terrible cold while I get them. They're right on the table here."

As Emily entered the kitchen, she saw Robert piling logs on the fire. "Good day, Emmy," he said, smiling at her.

She looked at him in surprise. Was it her imagination, or was Robert being unusually nice to her lately? He'd always been kind enough, she supposed, except when he was teasing her or acting like her big protector. Was he showing her more attention now because of Caroline? Or was he trying to hide some kind of secret? "Good day," she replied stiffly.

"There you go, dear," said Mistress Babcock, carefully placing a half-dozen eggs into Emily's basket. "I wish I had more to give you."

"Oh, these will do nicely," Emily replied. "Thank you kindly." She reached into the pocket of her cloak and brought out the jar. "My mother sent this for you," she said.

But as Emily held out the jar, she realized that she'd brought out the piece of black cloth as well.

"You must be doing some mending at your house," said Mistress Babcock, nodding toward the wool square as she took the jam.

"Uh, yes, ma'am," Emily said. She started to stuff the square back into her pocket, but then she thought better of it.

She turned to Robert, who was brushing wood dust off his hands. "Look what I found this morning," she said. "It was in the bushes outside our kitchen window. You see, there was someone out there last night after all."

43

Mistress Babcock gasped. "A thief, no doubt," she said. "There are many hungry people about town these days. Perhaps your father should—"

"I'll walk Emily home, Mother," Robert said quickly. He strode toward the door, his dark brows furrowed. "That way, we can be sure she gets there safely."

"Goodness, yes," Mistress Babcock said. "I won't be keeping Emily, or her family might be worried. Good-bye, Emily!"

"Good-bye," Emily said. It seemed she hardly had time to curtsy again before she was out on the street in front of the house with Robert. And he looked very upset.

"What were you talking about in there?" Robert demanded, his eyes flashing angrily. "Let me see that piece of cloth."

Emily drew herself up taller. "I will not," she said. "You're being extremely rude."

"Just give the square to me," Robert said. "Only for a moment. Please, Emily. I must see it."

"Oh, all right," Emily grumbled, handing him the cloth. "But I want it back."

Robert turned the wool square over in his hands. "It is as I feared," he said with a sigh.

Emily frowned. Did Robert recognize the cloth? Maybe he knew the identity of the man with the scar! "Robert, do you—" she began.

"Hush!" Robert said, looking over his shoulder. "It's not safe to talk. I'm taking you straight home."

"Why are you acting so strangely, Robert?" Emily asked, hurrying to catch up with him. "And why do you always say you're taking me home? What were you doing at the Common last night, anyway? Do you know that man who was at our window? And—"

Robert threw up his hands. "Enough!" he

said. He stopped in the street and whirled around to face Emily. "I've never known a young maid who asked so many questions. But I can tell you one thing—it would be much safer for you and me and your whole family if you kept quiet about that man you're so sure you saw in the window. You'll have to trust me."

Emily shrank back in surprise. *Trust* Robert? She didn't know what to think. She'd lived next door to Robert Babcock since she was practically a baby. But why was he being so mysterious now? Was her family in danger of the man with the scar? What if he wasn't a thief, after all? What if he was a British spy?

Emily's head was spinning. If the man with the scar was indeed a spy, then maybe he had been looking for Robert. Hadn't he followed them both back from the Common? And Robert had recognized the cloth from the stranger's cloak.

Then Emily's heart seemed to drop in her chest. Robert had gone to that secret meeting last night at her house! Had he told the awful man with the scar everything her father and his friends had talked about?

"Emily, will you give me your word that you won't say anything to anyone?" Robert asked.

Emily didn't answer. Instead, she ran all the way to her house, leaving Robert open-mouthed in the middle of the street.

5

"WHERE IS FATHER?" EMILY ASKED Caroline, her chest heaving as she burst through the door. "I need to talk to him right away!"

"Whoa, there!" Caroline said, laughing. She took the basket of eggs from Emily. "What have you gotten yourself all in a fit about this time?"

Emily ignored her. "I must speak to Father. It's about something very important."

"I'm sorry, my dear, but you will just have to wait," said Mistress Parker. She began to crack the fresh eggs against a bowl. "Your father is seeing a patient in his office."

Emily groaned and slumped onto a stool.

Her father often saw sick people at a moment's notice.

I'll talk to him as soon as he comes in to breakfast, Emily told herself. With a sigh, she unbuttoned her cloak and went over to the far corner of the kitchen to hang it up.

But there was already another coat hanging on the peg. It was a dark wool cloak with a large tear in the sleeve!

Emily gasped and nearly dropped her own cloak. The strange man with the scar was in their house at this very minute! And father could be in danger!

Emily tossed her cloak aside and rushed out of the kitchen, as her mother and sister looked up in surprise. *I must get to Father's office right away!* she thought wildly.

She rushed down the hall to the small room that had been built onto the back of her family's house. As soon as she neared the door, she reached out to knock, but she dropped her hand quickly when she heard voices.

Emily put her ear against the heavy wooden door. Someone was moaning loudly, and it wasn't her father. It had to be the owner of the cloak.

She leaned down and squinted into a small hole below the iron latch. She could just see a man with a mean-looking scar on his cheek, sitting in a large wooden chair. A long white bandage was wound around his chin and tied at the top of his head. Emily thought he looked like a very large rabbit with very long, floppy white ears.

"Oooohhh," the man groaned. "Me toof."

"There now, Mister Andrews," Dr. Parker said. He adjusted the bandage. "You'll soon be feeling much better. I've taken that troublesome tooth straight out. Though I must say I am surprised," he added, "that you did not visit

Mister Wells down at the forge. He usually sees to bad teeth."

Emily clapped a hand to her mouth. *Oh, no!* she thought. *I've made a terrible mistake! The poor man came to see Father because he had a toothache!* How could she have been so foolish? Maybe she did have an overactive imagination.

She was about to start back to the kitchen when she heard Mister Andrews say in a muffled voice, "The blacksmith was out this morning. I went straight to the forge at daybreak, the moment I began to be tormented by this merciless pain."

"Well, it was no trouble to see you myself," said Dr. Parker.

Emily frowned. She had seen the man with the scar at their window last evening. If Mister Andrews's tooth had begun to hurt just a short time ago, then why had he been lurking

around their house hours earlier?

Once again she squinted through the tiny hole under the latch. Dr. Parker was readjusting the bandage around Mister Andrews's face. "So what brings you to Boston, Mister Andrews?"

"I journeyed here from Philadelphia to be at my poor aunt's deathbed," the man replied. "She has no one else to look after her." His voice was muffled again.

"And who might this woman be?" Dr. Parker asked. "Perhaps she is one of my patients."

"Oh, no," Mister Andrews said quickly. "She lives in the north end of town."

"I often travel to visit the sick," said Emily's father. "Now what is your aunt's name? And where in the north end does she live? I know that area well."

Mister Andrews hesitated. "Her name is

Mary," he replied. "Mary Andrews. She lives on Salem Street. Number seventeen, I believe."

Dr. Parker shook his head. "You are right, my friend. I do not know any Mary Andrews. But perhaps I might be of service—"

"That is quite unnecessary, thank you," Mister Andrews said quickly. "My aunt will not allow any physicians near her bedside. She will see none but the clergy."

"I understand," said Dr. Parker. "But let me know if she has a change of heart."

The stranger nodded. "I will indeed."

"Tell me, my friend," said Dr. Parker. "How is it that you were allowed into Boston? The British stop and question everyone who wishes to enter or leave the town."

Mistress Andrews waved his hand. "Ah, I slipped one of the soldiers a few coins." He leaned forward, and Emily could just hear him add in a low voice, "Dr. Parker, I understand that you hold—er, private meetings in your home from time to time."

"A few of my friends and neighbors gather here on occasion," Dr. Parker replied carefully. "For a pint or two and a bit of conversation."

Emily held her breath. Surely her father wouldn't invite this nosy stranger into their home for one of those meetings! She didn't trust Mister Andrews one single bit. Perhaps her imagination was taking over again, but she felt sure that this man was up to no good. What would happen if she marched into her father's office right now and announced that Mister Andrews was a Tory spy?

No, Emily decided. She didn't have any real proof. But—

Just then, Emily heard footsteps coming down the hall. Quickly, she jumped away from the office door.

"Emily!" Mistress Parker said sharply when she spotted her. "What are you doing back here? Didn't I tell you that your father was not to be disturbed?"

"Yes, ma'am," Emily said meekly.

"Now come along," her mother said, guiding Emily back down the hall. "We'll start our breakfast without your father. Besides, I need you to buy a few things at the market this morning." She glanced sideways at Emily. "I trust you will arrive home before nightfall this time?"

"Yes, ma'am," Emily said. "I'll fetch the basket."

She entered the main room and hurried straight to the small writing desk in the corner. Rummaging through the desk, she found a quill pen, and inkwell, and a scrap of paper. *Seventeen Salem Street,* she wrote quickly. She blew on the paper to dry the ink, then picked up a large woven basket and stuffed the note at the bottom. She might need the address for evidence against Mister Andrews someday.

Half an hour later, Emily headed down the stone walk toward the front gate, deep in thought. Her father had never appeared at the breakfast table, and Mister Andrews's cloak was still hanging on the peg in the kitchen. What had they been talking about for such a long time in the back office?

"Emily!" a voice called. "Wait!"

Emily turned to see Maggie running down the street toward her. "'Twas some fine mess you left me in last night at the Common," she said when her friend had caught up.

Maggie looked concerned. "Oh, Em, I'm so sorry," she said, still panting a bit. "Did something terrible happen?"

"No," Emily said. "But—"

Maggie touched her arm. "Emily, I do very

much want to hear your story. But there's something very odd going on at the Common, and I thought that you should see it. I ran straight up here to fetch you."

"But what—?" Emily began again.

"There's no time to waste," Maggie said, breaking into another run. "Follow me!"

6

EMILY LIFTED HER SKIRTS AND RAN beside Maggie toward Boston Common. After several minutes of cutting through the narrow streets, Emily grew impatient. "Maggie," she huffed as a man on horseback passed them, "won't you tell me what it is you're bringing me to see?"

"We're nearly there," said Maggie, slowing her pace. "Come on, let's walk now. We need to look as though we're out for a morning stroll, in case the lobsterbacks see us. They have a sentry on duty, you know."

"I do indeed," Emily said, remembering the sentry she'd met last night.

Catching their breath, the two girls walked

along the Common until they had almost reached the spot where Emily had been stopped by the British soldier.

Maggie put a finger to her lips and drew Emily behind a row of hedges. "Look!" she whispered, pointing toward the British camp.

All Emily could see were lines and lines of red-coated soldiers, drilling on the green. A young boy carried the British flag, followed by others playing drums and fifes. Beyond the marching soldiers were long rows of small tents, tied horses, and smoldering campfires.

"That lad over there, just beyond the sentry," Maggie said. "Isn't that your neighbor, Robert Babcock? The one who calls himself a Patriot?"

Emily's mouth dropped open as she peered through the branches of the hedges. "It is, indeed," she said finally. "And it looks like he's having a serious conversation with those two British soldiers."

"What do you suppose he is doing in the British camp?" Maggie asked.

Emily shook her head. "I haven't the foggiest notion," she said.

"Perhaps he is going to enlist in the King's army," Maggie suggested.

"It's possible," Emily said. "But it's even more likely that Master Robert is a Tory spy!"

Maggie gasped. "That's terrible!"

"Wait," Emily said. "There's more." She filled her friend in on all that had happened since the previous night, and told her about the mysterious man with the scar on his face.

"So," Emily finished, "I'm beginning to suspect that both this Mister Andrews and Robert Babcock are up to no good."

"Do you think they are working together?" Maggie asked.

Emily nodded. "I'm almost certain of that.

I think Mister Andrews was trying to spy on a meeting that was held at my father's house last night. I scared him away, but the rascal was snooping around again this morning. How would a stranger in town know that Father and his friends meet in secret?"

"Well, does Robert come to your house for those meetings?" Maggie asked.

"I'm afraid so," Emily said. "Most likely, he tells Mister Andrews everything. And the worst of it is, my sister Caroline is in love with that Tory spy!"

Maggie clapped her hands over her ears. "I don't want to hear anymore," she said. "What an awful mess!" She dropped her hands again. "Will you tell your father?"

"Of course," said Emily. "Just as soon as I get home."

"What do you suppose the men were talking about last night?" Maggie asked. She lowered her voice even more. "I've heard it said that General Washington is preparing to drive out the British by attacking Boston."

"That's not very likely," Emily said. "Father and Robert were talking about that very thing at supper. The Americans have few men, even fewer guns and cannon, and almost no powder."

Maggie glanced nervously over her shoulder. "My Aunt Josephine lives in the countryside, just outside Framingham," she whispered. "She says it's rumored that supplies are on the way to the American army from Fort Ticonderoga."

Emily frowned. "Fort Ticonderoga! But that's so far north, and it's the middle of winter. It would be a foolish plan."

"Perhaps you are right," Maggie said. "'Twas probably just wishful talk."

Emily gazed through the hedge again.

"Maggie, Robert's leaving the camp," she said. "And he's headed this way. Let's follow him!"

"Shouldn't you go straight home and tell your father Robert is a traitor?" Maggie asked doubtfully. "That's what I would do."

"He can't do anything with us watching him," Emily said. "And perhaps we can even catch him spying red-handed."

"All right," Maggie agreed. "But we'll have to be very careful." Robert walked to the gate, tipped his hat to the soldier on guard, and immediately turned onto Common Street. The girls followed close behind him, taking care to keep their faces as hidden as possible under their cloaks.

Robert continued on to Treamont Street, turned down Queen Street, and continued walking quickly until he reached King Street.

"He's heading toward Long Wharf," Maggie said.

"Good," said Emily. "Mother sent me to buy fresh oysters there anyway." *And I'm going to be late again,* she added to herself. But surely her mother would understand when she heard the whole story.

The girls stepped onto the huge wharf, which stretched a third of a mile out into Boston Harbor. Shops and warehouses lined one side of the wharf. Ships were tied along the other side. Crowds of people made their way down the middle, along with wagons and carts and horses. Long Wharf was one of the busiest places in Boston, even in winter.

"Mind we don't lose sight of Robert," Emily said, worried. She could just see him ahead. Suddenly, he stopped outside the door of the Green Dragon, one of the town's most popular taverns.

"Do you think he's going inside?" Maggie asked.

But Emily hardly heard her. A man with an ugly scar on his face, dressed in a dark cloak with a large tear in the sleeve, was just rounding the corner of the tavern. He was no longer wearing the rabbit-ears bandage around his head. In fact, he seemed to have made a miraculous recovery from his painful toothache. And he was headed straight toward Robert!

Now I have my proof, Emily thought. *Robert Babcock and Mister Andrews are spying for the British! And they're about to have a secret meeting at this very minute!*

7

"THAT'S HIM! THE MAN WHO WAS LURK-ing around our house!" Emily told Maggie excitedly. As she watched, Mister Andrews walked straight past Robert, pretending not to see him. "We *must* hear what they say to each other," she added.

"I don't think we'll be able to do that," Maggie said. "Your Mister Andrews has gone into the tavern."

"Fiddlesticks," said Emily. She watched in dismay as Robert followed the cloaked man through the door a few moments later. "Maybe we should go inside ourselves."

"Emily Parker!" Maggie sounded shocked. "We'll not be going into a tavern. There's a rough lot of sailors and other rude, noisy men inside. If my father or brothers ever saw me in there—"

"That's it!" Emily cried, clapping her hands. "We'll pretend we're looking for your brothers. They're probably still working down at the Rope Walks, so we won't really find them."

"I don't think that's such a good idea," Maggie said. But Emily was already at the tavern door.

The girls squeezed their way into the crowded, smoky tavern. "There's Robert," Emily whispered. "Over there, under the ship's clock. And Mister Andrews is with him."

"What if they see us?" Maggie asked anxiously.

"Shh!" Emily told her. "Follow me." She pulled Maggie behind a group of men who were standing near the wall. With luck, they would be able to hear Robert and Mister

Andrews from there.

Emily's young neighbor and the man with the scar were huddled together, speaking in low tones. "General Washington . . ." Emily heard Robert say. "West side of town . . ." Mister Andrews nodded.

Suddenly, a large, hairy hand clamped down firmly on Emily's shoulder. Another hand came down on Maggie. "And what have we here?" a man's voice said loudly. "Two little maids in a gentleman's establishment?"

Emily looked up. The man was very stout, with a powdered wig and an extremely red face.

"Please, sir, we . . . we . . ." Maggie began.

"We're looking for Sean and Joseph Sullivan," Emily put in quickly. "You see, they're my friend's brothers, and it's very important that they come home right away."

The large man threw back his head and laughed. "Home, eh? There's work for them to do, I reckon." Suddenly, he shouted to every-one in the tavern, "Where are Sean and Joseph Sullivan? The lads are wanted home by their sister here."

Maggie cringed under the man's beefy hand.

"No Sullivans here!" someone called. "Not yet, anyway." A few men laughed.

"We'd best be going, then," Emily said. Maggie was already trying to make her way toward the door.

As she left, Emily glanced back toward the clock to see whether Robert and Mister Andrews had noticed them—but the two men were already gone!

Emily hurried after Maggie. She couldn't believe those spies had escaped, right from under her nose! How had they gotten out of the tavern so fast? A back door, no doubt. Now it was too late to catch them spying red-handed.

"Now what will we do?" Emily said, after she had caught up with Maggie outside.

Maggie looked exasperated. "I know what you can do," she said firmly. "You can make haste to buy those oysters for your mother and go straight home. That's what I'm going to do. Your father and his friends will take care of Robert and Mister Andrews."

"I certainly hope so," Emily said, walking back down the pier. But would anyone believe her story? People were always saying she had a wild imagination.

I need one more piece of proof, she decided finally. *But what?*

THE GIRLS WERE HALFWAY BACK to the Common when Emily remembered the note in her basket.

"That's it!" she said excitedly.

"What?" Maggie said, looking puzzled.

Emily rummaged under the parcel of oysters and brought out the small piece of paper. "Mister Andrews gave my father this address this morning," she explained. She handed the note to her friend.

Maggie frowned. "*Seventeen Salem Street.* Why, that's very near my house, in the north end of town."

"He said that's where his aunt lives," Maggie said. "But there are many houses on Salem Street."

"Let's go there right now and knock on the door," Emily suggested eagerly. "We can say we have lost our way if anyone answers."

Maggie hesitated.

"Please say you'll do it," Emily said. "It's the only way we can find out whether Mister Andrews was lying." She glanced sideways at Maggie. "And if you won't go with me, I'll just have to go myself."

"Sometimes I believe you go looking for trouble, Emily Parker," Maggie said with a sigh. "But I'll play spy again if you're truly certain we must."

Emily smiled. "I knew you'd say yes!"

A few minutes later, the girls passed the Sullivans' small wooden house on North Street. "'Tis not much farther," Maggie said.

Emily nodded. She didn't often visit the north end, except for the times she went to visit Maggie.

Under her breath, Emily counted the number of houses on Salem Street. "Seventeen," Emily said, as they reached a large, imposing stone house.

"It looks as though Mistress Andrews is quite well off," said Maggie.

"'Tis a lovely house," Emily agreed, gazing up at the many windows. "Shall we go through the gate?"

Suddenly, they heard a pounding of hooves. Emily covered her face with the side of her hood as the air filled with dust.

"Stand away!" a man shouted.

Emily jumped back onto the walk just as an elegant carriage drawn by four fine black horses pulled up in front of the house. A footman sprang down immediately from his perch on the back of the carriage and opened the door for the passenger.

"Mind your step, Mistress Andrews," the footman said.

"That's her!" Emily told Maggie excitedly.

A moment later, a haughty-looking older woman emerged from the carriage and swept by the footman. She did not seem to notice the two girls staring at her from the walk.

A servant girl ran out of the house and curtsied to Mistress Andrews. "Good day, ma'am," she said. "Do you have any parcels that need carrying?"

Mistress Andrews waved a hand as she continued toward the door. "Fetch them from the carriage," she said. "And don't dawdle. I'll need those things to wear this evening at General Percy's dinner party."

"She doesn't look very sick to me," Maggie murmured, as the woman disappeared into the house.

Emily shook her head. "Mister Andrews was definitely lying. And did you hear his high and mighty aunt say she's going to General Percy's house this evening? The Andrewses *must* be Tories!"

"Will you talk to your father now?" Maggie asked.

Emily nodded. "I won't waste another minute. Who knows what Robert and Mister Andrews were plotting in the tavern this afternoon?"

With that, Emily said good-bye to her friend and walked briskly home. As she had expected, her mother was very cross when Emily arrived. It was already late afternoon.

"And where have *you* been, miss?" Mistress Parker asked, her hands on her hips. "Did I not tell you to come straight home with those oysters? And where is my cornmeal?"

"Cornmeal?" Emily repeated blankly.

Mistress Parker threw up her hands. "Emily Parker, I have a good mind to give you a taste of thimble pie," she said. "Perhaps a few raps with a hard thimble will knock some sense into your foolish head. Do you ever pay any mind to what I tell you?"

"I'm sorry, Mother," Emily said. "I'll go out again for the cornmeal. But I have something very important to tell everyone."

"I don't want to hear it," Mistress Parker said firmly, untying her apron. "Not one word.

I'll fetch the cornmeal for the pudding myself. There's some sort of trouble brewing, and your father is out at the tavern. I expect he'll be bringing men home to supper, and here we are with no hospitality to offer them." Putting on her heavy cloak, she went out the door, slamming it behind her.

Emily's face fell. Her father wasn't home! How was she going to tell him about Robert and Mister Andrews being Tory spies? Caroline looked up from the kitchen table, where she was rolling out biscuits. "Do you have another wild story for us, Emily?" she said. "What is it this time? Goblins at the window? A dreadful sea creature in Boston Harbor? Flying pigs on the Common?"

"'Tis nothing like that!" Emily said angrily, the blood rushing to her face. "If you must know, it's about your precious Robert Babcock. I have certain proof that he is a Tory spy! And he's been spying right here in this very house!"

Caroline sprang toward Emily, sending puffs of precious flour in all directions. "How dare you say such a thing!" she cried. "Robert is the most patriotic lad in Boston, no matter what side the rest of his family is on." She clenched her fists. "If I weren't a lady, I'd box your ears!"

"A lady?" Emily scoffed. "Just look at you, all covered in flour and your hair falling out of your cap!"

"Why, you—you—" Caroline sputtered. She suddenly burst into tears and ran out of the kitchen.

Just then, Emily heard voices and heavy footsteps at the front door. Her father was home!

She hurried out to the hall, determined to speak to him immediately, but she stopped short when she saw who was with her father. In the middle of the group of Dr. Parker's friends and neighbors stood Robert Babcock.

That snake, Emily thought angrily. *He's a true spy through and through.* She had a good mind to reveal his treachery right there in front of everyone. But then she thought of Caroline, upstairs crying her eyes out, no doubt. Her sister probably knew Robert better than anyone. What if, by some tiny chance, Emily was wrong about him?

"Is the supper ready, Daughter?" Dr. Parker asked.

"Not yet, Father," Emily answered.

Dr. Parker nodded toward the kitchen. "We'll need to be eating early this evening," he said. "Perhaps your mother and sister could use your help."

Emily wasn't about to tell him that her mother was still out and Caroline was in hysterics, all because of her. "Yes, Father," she said, retreating to the kitchen.

An hour later, as darkness began to fall, Emily, Caroline, and Mistress Parker ate in silence at the kitchen table. The men had taken up all the chairs in the main room, and they appeared to be talking about something very important. *Robert is drinking up every word,* Emily thought hopelessly. Should she tell her mother now? But Caroline was sitting right there, red-eyed, and she'd say Emily was lying.

A few moments later, Dr. Parker poked his head into the kitchen. "Wife, I need to speak with you a moment," he said.

Immediately, Mistress Parker walked over and listened to something her husband told her in a low voice. When he left again, Emily's mother turned to the girls.

"Caroline, Emily, it's time for bed," she said.

Caroline nodded. "Yes, Mother," she answered, rising from the table. Mistress Parker took the candle from the table and headed out of the kitchen.

Emily reluctantly followed her mother and sister. But as she climbed the stairs to her bedroom, she looked back down at the men in their meeting. In the firelight, every one of their faces, even Robert's, looked worried and serious.

Emily knew they were talking about the war. She was nearly certain that Robert Babcock would reveal what he heard to Mister Andrews and the British soldiers. And then every man around that table, including her own father, would be in grave danger.

8

A S SOON AS EMILY WAS SURE THAT Caroline was asleep, she left the warm four-poster bed and slipped her feet into her soft leather mules. *I must warn Father and the others about Robert,* she told herself.

Shivering, Emily tiptoed toward the door. If she opened it, it would make a frightful noise. She could barely make out the men's voices, but they were too muffled for her to determine what was being said.

Then Emily remembered the hole in the floorboards, just next to the wardrobe. She crept over and knelt down to put her ear against the wood floor.

But even listening through the hole wasn't

much use. The men seemed to be composing some sort of message. Emily heard someone say something about knocking on a door. Another man suggested ham for supper.

Emily frowned. What could they possibly be talking about? Then she heard a younger person say clearly, "Why trust a stranger at the river to carry the message? I'll take it across the Charles to General Washington's headquarters in Cambridge myself."

Robert! Emily froze in horror. She couldn't let that traitor carry anything anywhere! She jumped up and ran to the wardrobe for her dressing gown.

But as she reached for the latch, she heard a slight creaking sound. *A rat,* Emily thought with a shudder. But this was no time to be cowardly. She took hold of the latch once again, but the door of the wardrobe refused to open.

That's odd, Emily told herself, struggling

with the bolt. It was almost as though there was someone inside refusing to allow her to open the wardrobe.

Emily's blood suddenly turned cold in her veins. "Father!" she cried. "Father, come quickly! Help!"

Caroline sat bolt upright in bed, clutching the bedclothes to her chest. "What?" she said, sounding frightened. "What is it?"

Emily didn't answer. She ran to the bed, yanked down the quilt, and reached for the long-handled brass bed warmer. As she did, the wardrobe doors flew open and Mister Andrews stepped out!

At the same moment, Emily's father ran into the bedroom, followed by Robert and the rest of the men.

Emily whirled around. "There he is!" she gasped, pointing with the bed warmer.

Sure enough, Mister Andrews was plastered against the wardrobe, looking terrified. The men lunged toward him, shouting. "Unhold me!" he told one of the men. "I need to see the doctor. I'm a patient of his. You can ask him yourself!"

The men looked at each other in confusion, and Emily's mother hurried into the room. Her face was very white.

"You can explain the story to Mister Collins down at the gaol," Dr. Parker told Mister Andrews angrily. "What in blazes are you doing in my daughter's chambers?"

Mister Andrews began to struggle again, and the men were soon busy trying to subdue him. Mister Flanders, one of their neighbors, took the bed warmer from Emily and started toward the wardrobe.

The intruder tried to break away once again, but Dr. Parker and the other men pinned him securely against the wardrobe.

"What shall we do with this rascal?" one of the men asked.

Everyone began to talk at once. Suddenly, over all the noise, Emily heard an urgent pounding. Someone was shouting downstairs at the front door. She slipped out of the room and hurried down the stairs.

"Open up, in the name of liberty!" a voice was calling urgently. "For mercy's sake, answer this door!"

Emily rushed forward, her heart thundering in her chest. She undid the latch and opened the door just a crack, but the person on the other side pushed in the door roughly and ran past Emily.

It was young Christopher Smith, who worked in the tavern down the road. "Where are your father and the others?" he demanded.

Emily hesitated. *What should I say?* she thought. Then there was another commotion from upstairs, and Christopher bounded up the steps two at a time. "They're coming!" he shouted. "Two British officers are on their way to arrest all in this house for unlawful assembly! Make haste, they're nearly here!"

With that, Christopher rushed past Emily again, jumped on the horse he'd left outside the gate, and galloped off.

Moments later, Emily pressed herself against the wall as the men began pounding down the stairs and past her toward the front door. They stopped only to gather their coats and hats before running out into the night. A few went out through the kitchen.

Where's Robert? Emily asked herself frantically. Had he gotten away? Had he been the one who alerted the British about the meeting in her family's house? Would he truly have betrayed her father and the other men?

Then Emily's eyes fell upon the piece of

paper lying next to the candle on the table. It was the message for General Washington! And it would certainly never do for the British officers to find it when they came to search the house.

Emily snatched the note from the table. It said:

Put down your gun,

Powder your wig,

And give forty-three knocks

Upon the door frame

So that you may have ham for supper.

EMILY STARED AT THE PIECE OF paper in her hand. *How very odd,* she told herself. It was like a child's rhyme.

Whatever its meaning, Emily knew from what the men had been saying that the note would be very important to General Washington. And Robert Babcock had been very anxious to get his hands on it.

Without another moment's hesitation, Emily ran to get her heavy dark shoes from the back hall. If General Washington needed this note, then he would have it. And she would carry the message herself, if need be. She knew her way to the river, even in the dark. And if someone stopped her, surely she could tell some sort of story.

Suddenly, not too far off in the distance, Emily heard the pounding of hooves and a horse's whinny. The soldiers were very close and there was no time to lose. Quickly, she opened the door and slipped out into the night, praying the soldiers would find her father upstairs in bed, pretending to be fast asleep.

And by the time anyone discovered she was missing, she'd be well on her way to Cambridge.

9

EMILY HURRIED DOWN WINTER STREET, the mysterious message tucked safely in the toe of her shoe. The cold air stung her eyes and pierced straight through her dress. *If I keep moving quickly I'll be warm enough,* she told herself. She wished she had remembered to grab her cloak in her haste to leave.

She tried to think ahead to every stage of her journey. Getting to the river would be the easiest part. Under cover of darkness, taking back streets, she would be quite safe. Finding someone to take her by boat to Cambridge would be more difficult, and crossing the Charles would probably be risky as well. British soldiers patrolled the waterfront day and night.

Clip clop, clip clop. Emily was sure her shoes were making an unusually loud clatter as she ran across the cobblestones. The sound seemed to echo through the frosty air. *Someone will hear me,* she thought in alarm.

Suddenly, she stumbled, and fell forward onto the street.

Emily quickly got up again, and brushed the dirt from her smarting hands. Then she realized she was missing a shoe, the one that had held the note.

Emily hobbled around on the cobblestones until she found the shoe. Luckily, the note was still inside. *I'll have to put it somewhere safer,* she told herself. She tucked the folded piece of paper carefully under the nightcap she had forgotten to remove in her haste to leave the house.

Her knees were still stinging from her fall,

but she quickened her pace again. She had to arrive at General Washington's headquarters before Robert reached the British camp!

That was going to be impossible, Emily realized. It was a good deal farther to Cambridge than it was to the Common. But the sooner she reached General Washington, the sooner he could take action on the message she carried under her cap.

But what does the note really mean? Emily wondered as she neared the house where British General Percy was staying. Clearly, it was a message written in some sort of code.

She muttered the message once again under her breath. "Put down your gun, powder your wig." When she said the lines out loud, the words *gun* and *powder* came together. And hadn't her father said that the American army was well short of gunpowder? But she could make no sense of the wig. Or the forty-three knocks, for that matter. Why would anyone have to knock so many times?

Knocks! Hadn't Robert mentioned a Colonel Knox that night at supper, when her father had changed the subject so quickly? Emily frowned as she dodged a large branch lying across the road. So it could be something about Colonel Knox and gunpowder. But why would one knock upon a door frame to get a ham?

Frame and ham. *That's it!* Emily thought excitedly. Framingham was the town where Maggie's Aunt Josephine lived, about twenty miles from Boston. And what about the rumor that supplies were on their way to the American army? From someplace up north. Fort Ticonderoga, Emily remembered.

Her mind continued to race. Had Colonel Knox brought precious gunpowder through the snow as far as Framingham? If so, then General Washington would soon have ammunition to fire upon the British in Boston!

But General Washington would never attack the city, Emily realized. It would be much too dangerous for all the people who lived there. Perhaps the number "forty-three" meant something. But what?

Still deep in thought, Emily turned at General Percy's house. Candles were ablaze in the windows, and she could hear loud, merry laughter and singing. *The dinner party,* she thought darkly. Mistress Andrews was probably in there, dancing a minuet at that very moment.

Suddenly, out of the darkness, someone came up behind Emily and clapped a hand over her mouth.

Terrified, Emily struggled against the person's grasp. "Let me go!" she tried to shout, but her words were too muffled for anyone to hear.

"Emily, it's me," a voice said quietly.

"Robert. Please don't be frightened. I'll let go of you now, if you promise not to make any noise."

Emily nodded angrily and twisted around to face Robert Babcock as he slowly dropped his hands. "I most certainly will make noise!" she told him. "I don't have to keep any promises to a traitor." She opened her mouth to call for help.

"Wait!" Robert said in a loud whisper. "If you cry out, someone in General Percy's house will hear you. The message you're carrying will fall into British hands."

"That's just what you want, isn't it, Robert Traitor Babcock?" Emily cried. She took a few steps away from him, ready to flee. "Well, if I am carrying any note, I'm not handing it over to you. I'm taking it straight to General Washington himself."

Robert took a deep breath. "Emily, it is too dangerous a journey for a young maid. The

British shoot at boats trying to cross the river to Cambridge. You wouldn't have a chance."

Emily looked at him with contempt. "I have as much of a chance as you, you Tory spy. How dare you put my father's life in danger?"

"Please trust me, Emily," Robert pleaded, stepping toward her. "I'm no Tory. And it is very urgent that General Washington receive that message at once. I can carry it more quickly than you. And what would your family think of me if I let you travel to Cambridge in the middle of the night? Please give me the note."

Emily folded her arms. "I won't," she said. "And if you dare try to take it from me, I'll— I'll—" She stopped, frowning. What *would* she do?

Robert sighed. "I don't need the note," he said. "I know what it says. I'll take you home, even though an important message will be delayed in reaching the Continental Army. But

I suppose that is but a trifle to a silly, selfish little miss like yourself." He reached out and grabbed the shoulder of Emily's dress.

"Unhold me!" Emily cried. "Will you ever stop trying to lead me like a goat? Let go, or I'll scream!"

Just then, the door of General Percy's grand house opened, and a tall figure holding a candle stepped outside. "What is the trouble out there?" a voice called.

Emily and Robert both froze. "Now see what you've done," Emily said, in a furious whisper. "Why don't you run over there to General Percy's servant and betray your friends and neighbors and Caroline?"

"I'd die first," Robert said quietly.

"What?" Emily turned to him in surprise. Did he really mean that? Or was this another one of his traitorous tricks?

The man with the candle unlatched the

gate and started toward them.

"I wish you would trust me, Emily," Robert said. "But if you will not, then tell General Percy's servant I came upon you and frightened you in the dark. They'll send me to sit in the gaol with that rascal Mister Andrews."

The servant had nearly reached them now. Emily hesitated, trying to decide what to do. If Robert was truly a Tory spy, he could walk straight into General Percy's house and deliver the message.

"I say, what is going on out here?" the man with the candle called. "Are you guests of the general?"

"Good luck, Emily," Robert said in a low voice. "And Godspeed to Cambridge."

Emily quickly made her decision. "Oh, 'tis something terrible!" she cried, running to meet the servant. "Two men have broken into my family's house down the road. They've caught one of them, but the other got away!" She covered her face with her hands and began to sob. "I was so frightened I ran straight out of the house!"

Robert stepped forward. "I was trying to bring Miss Parker home," he said. "But she is quite upset, as you can see."

Emily dropped her hands. "The other man, he went in that direction," she said, pointing toward the river. She sniffed loudly.

The servant gave Emily a kindly pat on the shoulder. "There, there, miss," he said. "We'll send you straight home in General Percy's carriage." He turned to Robert. "The thief went toward the river, you say?"

Robert nodded. "That's right. I'm sure I can catch him. If you'll see to Miss Parker—"

"But of course," the nice man said. Emily almost felt guilty for deceiving him. "Come along, miss."

As the servant led Emily toward the big house, Robert turned and bolted down the street toward the waterfront.

Please let it be the right decision, Emily thought. She wanted to believe Robert was on his way to General Washington's headquarters.

Had she been wrong to trust him?

10

AS GENERAL PERCY'S CARRIAGE PULLED up in front of the Parker's house, with Emily and the general's servant inside, Emily felt sick to her stomach. What had happened to her father when the British officers arrived? And whatever would her family say about her running into the night?

But just as Emily was emerging from the carriage, her heart pounding, Dr. Parker rode up to the house on horseback.

He jumped from the saddle and gave Emily a hug. "I'm thankful you're safe," he said. Mistress Parker and Caroline came running out of the house.

"I'm all right," Emily told everyone meekly.

Then she looked her father straight in the eye. "I was so scared when that awful second man came into my bedroom that I ran straight out of the house."

"Second man?" Caroline said, sounding confused.

Emily rushed on, hoping her father would understand. "Robert ran after me, and now he's chasing the other thief—"

Dr. Parker nodded. "I see."

"She was a very frightened maid indeed," the general's servant put in. "So I thought it best to bring her home immediately. The lad headed straight down to the river."

"Thank you for your kindness to our daughter," Dr. Parker said, reaching into his pocket for some coins. "We're happy to have Emily back safe. We've had a great deal of excitement here tonight."

The general's servant nodded and handed

the coins back to Dr. Parker. "Thank you, but it was no trouble, sir. Did they catch the rascal?"

"They did indeed," Dr. Parker told him. "He was ranting all the way down to the gaol about being on some sort of spy mission." He shook his head. "A far-fetched notion if I ever heard one."

The general's servant looked sympathetic. "What those scoundrels will say to avoid punishment at the stocks," he said. Then he stepped back into the carriage and told the driver to go.

As the carriage rattled down the street, Emily and her family went into the house.

Everyone immediately began fussing over Emily. Her mother went to make her a strong mug of tea, and Caroline brought her a blanket. "I was so worried about you," she said. "As soon as the British soldiers came and took that Mister Andrews away, we realized you were gone. Robert and Father went out looking for you."

"I know what you were trying to do," Dr. Parker said sternly. "Just before the soldiers arrived, Robert noticed the note was missing from the table. He was going to take it across the river himself. It was very foolish of you to try to deliver that message to General Washington."

Emily glanced at Caroline. "I wasn't sure I could trust Robert," she said, looking down at the floor. Then she told them the whole story, starting from the time she had first run into Robert at the Common.

Caroline looked shocked, but Dr. Parker let Emily finish.

"Well, Daughter, you were right about the message," he said finally. "Colonel Henry Knox has indeed brought forty-three cannon and a large supply of gunpowder by boat and oxcart through the snow from Fort Ticonderoga to Framingham. Word of his success reached Boston today. We knew General Washington would be most anxious to hear of the guns' arrival."

Emily looked over at her sister again. Caroline was listening, stone-faced, but she was twisting her hands nervously in her lap. Emily knew Caroline had never believed Robert was a traitor. But Emily still wasn't sure.

"And you were right about one other thing," Dr. Parker went on. "Young Robert Babcock has been spying."

Caroline gasped, and Emily felt the color drain from her face. *I should never have trusted him,* Emily told herself.

"However, Robert is a spy for the Patriot cause," Dr. Parker continued. "He has been feeding the British Army false information about a Patriot build-up of men and arms on the west side of Boston. Mister Andrews was Robert's British contact."

Emily began to breathe more easily. So that was what the two men had been discussing in the Green Dragon Tavern! She remembered Robert saying something about the west side of town.

"And as you can imagine," Dr. Parker finished with a smile," I was quite certain that our friend Mister Andrews did not really have such a terrible toothache that morning he showed up at our door."

Everyone had more questions for Emily, but Mistress Parker insisted that they be left until the morning. "Emily needs her rest now," she said.

Two hours later, Emily lay in her bed, still wide awake. Beside her, Caroline was pretending to sleep, but she, too, was staring silently into the darkness.

Emily knew her sister was waiting for Robert to come back, but it would be some time before they would have any news. It was a long, dangerous journey to Cambridge and back again.

Emily squeezed her eyes shut tighter. She couldn't stop thinking about Robert, either. She wished she had been able to go with him to deliver the message to General Washington. *It would have been such a great adventure,* she told herself with a yawn.

The next thing Emily knew, sunlight was streaming in through the opening in the bed-curtains. It was well past the time she usually woke up.

Quickly, she jumped out of bed and pulled on her clothes. She could hear her mother and Caroline preparing breakfast downstairs, and her father throwing logs on the fire.

For once, no one said anything to her about having overslept. In fact, no one talked very much at all. Caroline's face looked drawn and puffy as she poured fresh milk into a jug. Mistress Parker went about preparing the meal, her brow lined with worry. Even Emily's father was unusually silent, as he paced the floor in front of the fire.

Suddenly, the door burst open, and Robert Babcock stepped inside.

"Robert!" Caroline cried, rushing forward. "You're safe!"

Robert grinned. "Indeed I am," he said. "And General Washington sends his regards."

"Well done, lad," Dr. Parker said, slapping him on the back.

Emily's mouth dropped open. "You saw General Washington himself!" she exclaimed in awe.

"Well, not exactly," Robert said. He reached over to tweak her nose. "I delivered the message to one of his aides. But I told him all about you."

He's still treating me like a child, Emily thought, annoyed. But she had to admit, he had been very brave. And he certainly wasn't a Tory spy. "I'm sorry I doubted you," she told him, flushing a bit.

"No matter," said Robert, shrugging. "You were right about almost everything. But the important thing is, General Washington will soon have his guns."

"And the British will sail straight out of town," Emily said happily.

Dr. Parker smiled down at her. "I hope so, my daughter," he said. " We will just have to wait and see."

Emily smiled back. She had a feeling they wouldn't have to wait much longer before General Washington used the great guns from Fort Ticonderoga to drive the British from Boston.

And this time, she was right.